Aunt Eater's Mystery Vacation

Doug Cushman

SCHOLASTIC INC.

New York Toronto London Auckland Sydney
Mexico City New Delhi Hong Kong Buenos Aires

For
Jack & Carolynn
Prelutsky

All rights reserved. Published by Scholastic Inc., 557 Broadway, New York, NY 10012, by arrangement with HarperCollins Publishers. SCHOLASTIC and associated logos are trademarks and/or registered trademarks of Scholastic Inc.

ISBN 0-439-45499-9

12 11 10 9 8 7 6 5 4 3 2 1   3 4 5 6 7 8/0

First Scholastic printing, June 2003

Printed in the U.S.A.

Aunt Eater found a seat

and opened her book.

The waves were high.

The ferry swayed back and forth.

Suddenly, a big wave hit the ferry.

WHOOSH! CRASH!

Everyone looked sick.

All except Aunt Eater.

"What a fun ride," she said.

"But it is hard to read my mystery."

Just then the first mate

rushed on deck.

"Has anyone seen the captain?"

he cried.

"I can't find him anywhere!"

10

All the passengers just moaned.

"This sounds like a mystery,"

said Aunt Eater.

"I will help you

find the captain."

Aunt Eater and the first mate
searched the whole boat.
They looked on the upper deck.

They looked on the lower deck.

They looked in the engine room.

They even looked in the lifeboats.

They could not find

the captain anywhere.

"We will be landing soon,"
said the first mate.
"I must lower the anchor."
"Stop!" a voice cried.
"Do not lower the anchor!"
"That sounds like the captain!"
cried the first mate.
Aunt Eater rushed to the railing.
The first mate ran
to get a rope.

The first mate pulled the captain
back on deck.

"What happened?" asked Aunt Eater.

"A big wave knocked me overboard,"

said the captain.

"Thank you for saving me."

17

"Aunt Eater, would you like
to ring the bell?
We are about to reach the shore,"
said the captain.
"Oh yes!" said Aunt Eater.

"What an exciting way

to begin my vacation!"

Ding! Ding!

"ALL ASHORE!"

cried Aunt Eater.

19

Aunt Eater Follows a Sweater

Aunt Eater checked in

to the Hotel Bathwater.

"We are happy to see you again,"

said the hotel detective, Mr. Bundy.

"It is good to be back,"

said Aunt Eater.

"Shiny! Shiny!"

squawked Pat, the mynah bird.

"No, no!" said Aunt Eater.
"Do not take the buttons
off my sweater.
Here is a nice shiny nickel."

22

The bellhop took

Aunt Eater's bags to her room.

Aunt Eater sat down

and opened her book,

but she was so tired from her trip,

she fell asleep.

She dreamed

she was a great detective.

She followed a dark figure

who left giant footprints.

The figure reached out

its bony hands....

"Help! Help!" cried a voice.

Aunt Eater woke up.

She heard the cry again.

"Someone is in trouble!" she said.

Aunt Eater ran out into the hallway.

25

"Someone stole my diamond ring,"

cried a woman in a green dress.

"I went into the bathroom

to powder my snout.

When I came out,

my ring was gone!

It was right there on the table!"

"I will call Mr. Bundy,"

said Aunt Eater.

"He will solve your mystery."

When Mr. Bundy came, he asked,

"What happened, Miss Wainscot?"

"Someone stole my ring,"

cried Miss Wainscot.

"Many things have been missing

at the hotel lately,"

said Mr. Bundy.

"But we have no clues.

Who can the thief be?"

"This is a *real* mystery,"

said Aunt Eater.

"I will get my sweater

and help you look for clues."

Aunt Eater went to her room
to get her sweater.
But her sweater was gone!
"Goodness!" she said.
"Now *I* am missing something!"

She saw a piece of yarn

on the windowsill.

"Oh my! My sweater

has come undone!" Aunt Eater cried.

"Maybe if I follow the yarn,

it will lead me to the thief."

She followed the yarn

down to the lake, past a bench,

around a tree, into the garden,

and there was Pat, the mynah bird.

Next to him were many shiny things—
paper clips, nickels,
big silver buttons, a silver pin,
and a diamond ring!

"So *you* are the thief,"

said Aunt Eater.

"Shiny! Shiny!" Pat squawked.

Aunt Eater took everything

to the hotel.

"You found my ring!"

cried Miss Wainscot.

"Well, it looks like

you solved this mystery,"

said Mr. Bundy.

"Thank you," said Aunt Eater.

"Now I am going to my room

to try to read my book."

Aunt Eater Tastes Some Soup

The next morning

Aunt Eater took a walk

in the garden.

She stopped near a bench.

"This is a lovely spot

to read my mystery," she said.

Then she saw a package

on the bench.

"What could this be?" she asked.

"There it is!" cried a voice.

"Hello, Professor Slagbottom,"

said Aunt Eater.

"Is this your package?"

"Yes," said the Professor.

"I am so forgetful."

"In this package is the leg bone

of the rare Swinesaurus,"

he said.

"It is the prize bone

in my dinosaur collection."

39

"Here you are," said Aunt Eater.

"Thank you,"

said Professor Slagbottom.

"I must be off."

Aunt Eater opened her book

and began to read her mystery.

Just as Aunt Eater

finished Chapter 4,

Professor Slagbottom

ran back into the garden.

"It's gone! It's gone!" he cried.

"What is gone?" asked Aunt Eater.

"My bone! My rare bone!"

said the Professor.

"I cannot find it!"

"This is a mystery,"

said Aunt Eater. "Let's think.

Where did you go this morning?"

"Hmm," said Professor Slagbottom.

"First I went to breakfast.

Then I went into the garden

and down to the lake.

Then I went to the kitchen.

Then I went back to my room."

"We will look in the kitchen first,"

said Aunt Eater.

"Have some soup," said Cook.

Aunt Eater took a sip of the soup.

"I do not want to complain,"

she said,

"but this soup is awful."

"It is the worst soup

I have ever tasted,"

said the Professor.

"Oh dear," said Cook.

"It must be the soup bone.

It was very big."

"Let me see the bone,"

said Aunt Eater.

Cook took the lid off the soup pot.

"That is my bone!"

cried the Professor.

"I am so forgetful.

I must have left it in the kitchen."

"A bone is a bone," said Cook.

"Professor Slagbottom,"
said Aunt Eater,
"I think you have made
another discovery."
"What is that?" asked the Professor.
"That dinosaur bones do not make
good soup," said Aunt Eater.

Aunt Eater Finds an Ending

After lunch

Aunt Eater was at the lake.

She was reading her book.

When she looked up,

she saw a strange woman

sneak up to the back door.

She had a notebook in her hand.

"Hmm," said Aunt Eater.

"She looks like someone

from one of my mystery books."

Aunt Eater followed her.

Aunt Eater saw

a piece of paper fall out

of the woman's notebook.

Aunt Eater picked it up

and read it.

"My goodness!" said Aunt Eater.

"She is a thief!

Maybe I can find the painting

and take it to Mr. Bundy."

So now you know my story.
I was the one who stole the famous painting "Still Life with Cabbage and French Fries." I hid it with the dinner plates at the hotel.

Aunt Eater raced into the kitchen.

She looked inside every cupboard.

She even looked in the drawers

and inside the pantry.

There was no painting.

54

Mr. Bundy came into the kitchen.

"What are you looking for?" he asked.

Aunt Eater told him

all about the strange woman

and showed him the paper.

"We must find her," Mr. Bundy said.

Aunt Eater took Mr. Bundy
to the back door.
"This is where I saw her,"
said Aunt Eater.
"This door goes
into the hotel library,"
said Mr. Bundy.

Suddenly they heard CRASH!

They ran into the library.

Books were everywhere.

In the middle of the room

was the strange woman.

"I can't find my ending!"

the woman cried.

"Ending?" asked Mr. Bundy.

"I came to the hotel

to finish my new story,"

said the woman,

"and now I have lost the ending!"

"Is this it?" asked Aunt Eater.

"Yes," cried the woman.

"Thank you!"

Suddenly Aunt Eater said,

"I know who you are.

You are Edna Herring,

the famous mystery writer.

You are my favorite author.

I have been trying to finish

one of your books

since I arrived at the hotel.

I *love* mysteries."

"So do I," said Miss Herring.

"Aunt Eater has solved two mysteries
since she came here,"
said Mr. Bundy.
"You have?"
said Miss Herring.

"You must tell me all about them.

Let's order some tea

and talk about mysteries."

"That is a lovely idea,"

said Aunt Eater.

And that is what they did.